LISA GRAFF
PICTURES BY JASON BEENE

Sophie Simon
Solves Them All

SQUARE
FISH

FARRAR STRAUS GIROUX
NEW YORK

To Melissa, a bona fide smarty-pants

SQUARE
FISH

An Imprint of Macmillan

Library of Congress Cataloging-in-Publication Data
Graff, Lisa (Lisa Colleen), 1981–
    Sophie Simon solves them all / Lisa Graff ; pictures by Jason
Beene.
        p.   cm.
    Summary: Sophie Simon, a third-grade genius, wants a graphing
calculator so she can continue to study calculus while she rides the bus
to school, but her parents are more concerned that she does not have
any friends.
    ISBN: 978-1-250-02898-3
    [1. Genius—Fiction.   2. Friendship—Fiction.   3. Schools—
Fiction.]   I. Beene, Jason, ill.   II. Title.

PZ7.G751577So 2010
[Fic]—dc22

                                                            2009041454

Originally published in the United States by Farrar Straus Giroux
First Square Fish Edition: September 2012
Square Fish logo designed by Filomena Tuosto
Book designed by Jay Colvin
mackids.com

2   4   6   8   10   9   7   5   3

AR: 3.9 / LEXILE: 680L

Contents

Who's Who   1

A Genius with a Problem   3
Check Marks and Squeegees   15
Piranhas and Pet Stores   34
Very Ugly Hats   51
The Lemur at the Pool Party   70

Sophie Simon's Encyclopedia of Things She
    Can't Believe You Don't Know Already   95
How to Make Madagascar Ground
    Boa Taffy   100

Who's Who

1. **Sophie Simon:** The smartest girl in the third grade (possibly the world)
2. **Mr. and Mrs. Simon:** Like to refer to their daughter as their "darling little sausage omelet"
3. **Mr. St. Cupid:** The dumbest teacher in all of Eisenberg Elementary (possibly the world)
4. **Owen Luu:** Likes things clean, quiet, and bland
5. **Mrs. Luu:** Likes things chaotic, loud, and spicy
6. **Daisy Pete:** Give her an inch, and she'll trip all over it
7. **Mr. and Mrs. Pete:** Own Petes' Pet Store. Want their daughter to be a star ballerina
8. **Madame Robespierre:** Teaches ballet with an iron fist
9. **Julia McGreevy:** Wants to be a famous journalist when she grows up. Wants to be a mathlete never
10. **Professor McGreevy:** Can't stop talking about math
11. **Lenny the Lemur:** A ring-tailed lemur

A Genius with a Problem

Every morning as they walked to the bus stop, Sophie Simon and her parents had the same conversation.

"Have fun at school today, lamb chop," her mother would say, straightening out Sophie's blouse.

And Sophie would wrinkle her cute button nose at her mother and tell her, "School is not for fun. It's for learning."

But that Friday morning, instead of simply patting Sophie on the head and nodding, Sophie's parents did something that surprised her.

"Snickerdoodle," Sophie's father replied, "your

mother and I have been thinking. Perhaps today you might try to make some friends."

Sophie tugged at the straps of her backpack. "No, thank you," she said. "I don't need friends."

"But, walnut," Sophie's mother said, taking hold of her hand as they crossed the street. "Don't you even want one or two friends? All of the other children seem to have them."

"That's true," said Sophie's father.

Sophie scowled at her parents.

She was *not* like other children.

Sophie Simon was a *genius*.

By the time Sophie Simon was two, she could recite the alphabet backwards and forwards. The Russian alphabet.

By the time she was four, Sophie had dismantled her parents' broken toaster and turned it into a working radio.

And at the age of seven, Sophie had successfully performed open-heart surgery on an earthworm in the front yard.

Since earthworms have five hearts each, this was a pretty difficult task.

You would think that having a genius for a daughter would have made Sophie's parents delighted.

It did not.

Aileen and Maxwell Simon worried that their daughter wasn't "well-adjusted."

They were always quoting the famed child expert Doctor Wanda, who told parents on her TV show that the worst thing they could do was push their children to grow up too quickly.

To Sophie's parents, growing up too quickly meant doing anything Sophie found interesting.

If Sophie crafted a working robot out of

toothpicks and rubber bands, her parents sighed and told her that well-adjusted children made birdhouses.

If Sophie taught herself to speak Japanese from a textbook, her parents shook their heads and said that well-adjusted children spoke pig Latin.

And if Sophie composed her own concerto on the neighbor's grand piano, her parents rubbed their temples and complained that well-adjusted children played the kazoo.

Sometimes Sophie wondered if maybe her parents weren't really her parents. Maybe, Sophie thought, she had been switched with another baby in the hospital. A well-adjusted baby. Maybe her real parents were out in the world somewhere right now, wondering why their daughter wanted to play with dolls instead of encyclopedias.

But really, Sophie knew that the people who walked her to the bus stop every morning *were* her real parents. Because Sophie had her mother's wavy hair, blond like straw. And she had her father's blue eyes, and the same curvy earlobes. So she most definitely had not been switched at birth.

Too bad.

"Gumdrop," Sophie's father said as they reached the bus stop. They were the first ones there, as usual. "Isn't that nice boy from your class having a birthday party this Sunday?"

"Why, yes," Sophie's mother said. "That charming little boy we met at parents' night. Owen Luu. The one who was afraid of paste. He seemed *extremely* well-adjusted."

Sophie rolled her eyes.

If Owen Luu was well-adjusted, then she was the president of Finland.

"That's the one," Sophie's father said. "An invitation for the party came in the mail last week. Wouldn't you like to go, marshmallow? It's going to be a 'birthday pool-party extravaganza.' There will be an eight-layer ice cream cake, a high-dive contest, and an old-fashioned taffy pull."

"Oh, peanut, doesn't that sound delightful?" her mother exclaimed. "It would be a perfect opportunity to make friends."

Sophie didn't answer. She had never been to a birthday party, and she never wanted to go to one, either. And she certainly didn't want any *friends*. Sophie knew for a fact that she didn't need friends.

Friends did things like hang from the monkey bars and trade stickers.

Friends told each other secrets and laughed at silly jokes.

Having friends sounded like a waste of time.

"You know," Sophie said, trying to change the subject, "you really don't have to walk me to the bus stop anymore. I'm old enough to come by myself."

"Oh, bean sprout!" her mother said. "We could never let you walk all this way by yourself!"

"It's three whole blocks!" her father agreed. "What if you got lost?"

At dinner the night before, Sophie had built a topographic map of Zimbabwe out of her mashed potatoes. She would *not* have gotten lost.

"Here, dumpling," her mother said. "I made some cupcakes for your lunch. Let me put them in your backpack." She tugged at Sophie's zipper.

"Mom," Sophie said, "I've told you. I don't like cupcakes."

Sophie's favorite dessert was flan, a Mexican custard that her parents said looked like refrigerated cat food.

"Don't be silly, graham cracker!" her mother

said as she opened Sophie's backpack. "All well-adjusted children like cup—"

She did not finish her sentence.

"Sophie!" she screeched, her head halfway inside the backpack.

"What?" Sophie's father asked. "What is it?"

"Oh, Maxwell, you won't believe what I found in our daughter's bag! It's a . . ." She pulled out the object, and her husband snatched it from her.

"No!" he gasped.

"Yes!" Sophie's mother cried.

"It's a textbook!"

"A *college* textbook!"

"Mom," Sophie said. "Dad. I—" But she didn't get a chance to explain.

"Advanced Concepts in Modern Calculus," her father read. "Oh, Aileen, just imagine! Our well-adjusted daughter, exposed to this . . . *educational material*! The kind of stuff most *adults* don't understand!"

Sophie's mother put a hand on his shoulder. "Now, Maxwell, calm down. We don't even know if this book belongs to Sophie. Someone could have slipped it into her bag without her noticing. Let's give her a chance to explain before we get so worked up." She turned to Sophie. "Sugarplum?"

Sophie shrugged. "I just wanted to look at it on the bus," she said. "That's all."

Sophie's mother sucked in her breath. "Sophie!" she cried. "All this time you promised you'd only spend your free time reading comic books!"

"May I have my book back?" Sophie asked. "I want to study before school starts."

"Oh, Maxwell!" Sophie's mother wailed, grabbing her husband's arm. "Where did we go wrong?"

Sophie's father was shaking his head. "You try so hard to be a good parent," he said. "And then you find out your eight-year-old daughter is studying *calculus*."

Sophie puffed out her cheeks.

Other children were beginning to join them at the bus stop.

"But calculus is interesting," she tried to explain.

Sophie's father pointed an angry finger at her. "Don't you tell me calculus is interesting, young lady. I happen to know that calculus is *not* interesting. Calculus is *math*."

Sophie's father was right about one thing. Calculus *was* math. A very complicated kind of math. It involved long equations with letters and numbers and symbols so confusing that most people avoided looking at them directly, in case their brains turned to mush. There were graphs and charts and formulas and silly words like *tangent*.

Sophie loved it. She loved it more than any subject she'd ever studied before. Sophie loved calculus the way other children love roller coasters and trips to Disneyland.

She stayed up past midnight studying under the covers.

She thought about equations while her parents made her watch TV.

She even dreamed about calculus.

But there was one problem.

If Sophie *really* wanted to study calculus, really and truly, she needed a special kind of calculator.

"Mom? Dad?" Sophie asked as the Number 17 bus appeared over the hill in the distance. "Will you buy me a graphing calculator? I want the Pembo Q-60. It's the latest model. It costs one hundred dollars."

There was a pause.

A very short pause.

And in that pause, Sophie imagined what it might be like to have parents who understood her.

Parents who said, "Yes, dear, of *course* you may have a graphing calculator. Would you like a new set of notebooks and some fresh pencils to go along with it?"

Parents who let her study in peace and stopped bothering her about pointless things, like making friends.

But then the pause ended.

"Oh, Maxwell!" Sophie's mother sobbed. "What would Doctor Wanda say?"

Sophie's father shook his head. "You try so hard to be a good parent," he said with a sniffle. "And then your eight-year-old daughter tells you she wants a *calculator*."

Sophie heaved a deep sigh.

"So you won't buy me a Pembo Q-60 then?" she asked.

"No," said her mother.

"Absolutely not," said her father.

The bus slowed to a stop at the corner.

"May I at least have my book back?" Sophie wondered.

"No," said her mother.

"Absolutely not," said her father.

"But it's from the library!" Sophie protested. "I have to return it."

"Oh, Maxwell!" Sophie's mother wailed. "Our little girl's been visiting the *library*!"

Sophie's father shook his head. "You try so hard to be a good parent . . ." he began.

But Sophie didn't hear the rest. The second the bus doors squeaked open, she leaped up the steps and plopped herself into the first empty seat.

As the bus pulled away from the corner, Sophie watched her parents' faces grow smaller and smaller, weeping as they clutched her calculus book. When they had finally become specks in the distance and then disappeared, she turned around and thought.

There had to be *some* way to get that calculator. But how?

Sophie Simon didn't know it, but at that very moment, there were three other third-graders on the Number 17 bus who were puzzling over problems of their own.

Doozies.

Dilemmas.

Submarine-size pickles.

It would have taken a *genius* to solve all four problems.

Too bad Sophie Simon only cared about one of them.

Check Marks and Squeegees

Daisy Pete sat at her desk in Mr. St. Cupid's third-grade class, tapping her pencil and staring at the list of rules on the wall.

There were lots of rules in Mr. St. Cupid's class.

There were normal ones.

No pushing
No hitting
No chewing gum

And strange ones.

No choking
No wearing orange socks
No talking about fungus

Whenever anybody did something Mr. St. Cupid didn't like, the teacher would add a new rule to his list.

So far the list of rules covered nineteen sheets of poster board and spread across three walls.

As Daisy stared at the list, the pencil she was tapping on her desk flew out of her hand and straight up into the air.

It landed—*ker-PLUNK!*—on the head of the girl who sat in front of her.

Sophie Simon.

Sophie was so busy reading the book she had hidden under her desk, she didn't even notice the pencil sticking out of her blond ponytail.

Daisy thought Sophie Simon was a little odd. All she ever did was read. And trying to talk to her was like riding a bicycle upside down.

It didn't make any sense.

No wonder Sophie Simon didn't have any friends.

Daisy leaned forward and plucked her pencil

out of Sophie's hair. Luckily, Mr. St. Cupid didn't notice. If he had, she would have gotten in trouble for breaking Rule number 138:

No pulling objects out of other students' heads

Daisy did not want to get in trouble.

Every time you broke a rule in Mr. St. Cupid's class, you got a check mark next to your name on the board.

If you got three check marks, you had to stay inside for final recess and clean the windows.

Daisy hadn't been outside for final recess once all year.

Daisy never broke rules on purpose. But she seemed to be especially good at getting into trouble in Mr. St. Cupid's class.

In fact, Daisy was responsible for creating thirty-six of the rules on Mr. St. Cupid's wall, including:

No spilling glitter on the rug
No falling over in your desk
No dropping your science book on your foot
No tripping over your science book

No tripping over your backpack
No tripping over your shoelaces
NO TRIPPING

Daisy Pete had a lot of problems when it came to tripping.

But somehow, that Friday afternoon, Daisy only had two check marks next to her name. If she could make it through the rest of math time without breaking any more rules, she would finally get to go outside for final recess.

Daisy wondered what it was like out there. She'd heard rumors there were ice cream sundaes and dodgeball.

She was pretty sure the dodgeball part was true, at least.

"If I had *five* onions," Mr. St. Cupid bellowed at the class, "and I ate *three*, what would I be *left* with?"

No one raised a hand.

No one ever raised a hand in Mr. St. Cupid's class.

Daisy thought this was because Rule number 3 on the wall was

No moving your arms

18

Most days, Daisy thought Mr. St. Cupid's rules were pretty stupid. But today, having rules didn't seem like such a bad idea. Daisy could think of some good ones for her parents.

No yelling
No lecturing

And, most important,

No forcing your daughter to dance in a ballet recital

Daisy had been trying to get out of her ballet recital for weeks.

She told her parents that she hated ballet, and that her dance teacher was meaner than an angry werewolf.

She told them that the thought of falling over in front of hundreds of people at a dance recital made her want to spew her lunch all over her frilly pink tutu.

She told them that if they forced her to dance in the recital at the Middlebury Performing Arts Center on Saturday, it would be *utterly unfair.*

But did Daisy's parents pay any attention when she told them those things?

They did not.

Daisy's parents told her that she probably just had stage fright.

They told her that, when she got up onstage, she'd be a star.

They told her that, once she was a star, the world would be her oyster, and she wouldn't be stuck working in a pet store all her life like they were.

Well, Daisy didn't want any oysters. And she loved Petes' Pet Store. She couldn't imagine anything better than working there forever.

But when it came to ballet class, Daisy's parents didn't hear a single thing she said. It made Daisy feel *absolutely powerless*.

Sometimes Daisy wondered if maybe her parents weren't really her parents. Maybe, Daisy thought, her real parents had been abducted by aliens just after she was born, and replaced with androids who didn't understand that going to ballet class was worse than having your nose hairs yanked out with pliers. Maybe her real parents were up in a spaceship right now, watching their daughter as they orbited the earth, cringing every time she had to put on a leotard.

But really, Daisy knew that the people who bought her dance shoes and picked her up from class every Tuesday after school *were* her real parents. Because Daisy had seen lots of movies about aliens, and her parents didn't do anything weird and alieny like drink mountains of sugar water or shoot lasers out of their eyeballs. So they most definitely had not been abducted.

Too bad.

Daisy was snapped out of her thoughts by something poking into her left elbow. She turned to look.

At the desk next to her, Julia McGreevy was holding a folded-up square of paper.

"For Owen," Julia whispered.

Julia McGreevy and Owen Luu were best friends. Julia sat at the desk to Daisy's left, and Owen sat at the desk to Daisy's right.

Daisy passed a lot of notes.

Today, though, Daisy thought about ignoring Julia. Note passing was against the rules. If Daisy got caught, it would mean no final recess for sure.

"Please?" Julia begged.

Daisy sighed and took the note.

But just as she was about to place it on Owen's desk, Daisy sneezed.

When Daisy sneezed, she dropped things.

Daisy dropped the note.

Owen stuck his leg out to the side like a stretched-out dish towel, trying to cover up the note. But it was too late.

"*Mister* Luu!" Mr. St. Cupid shouted. "*What* are you doing?"

"I-I'm not d-doing anything," Owen stuttered.

"*Stop stuttering!*" yelled Mr. St. Cupid. "Stuttering is not allowed in my class! New rule!"

Daisy gulped.

Mr. St. Cupid walked over to Owen's desk and glared down at him. "*Why* is your *leg* stuck out like that?"

"Um . . ." Owen said. "I'm, um, stretching?"

"Well, it's *distracting*!" Mr. St. Cupid bellowed. "From now on, *stretching* is not allowed in my class! *New rule!*"

Daisy grimaced.

"But I had a leg cramp," Owen said.

"*Leg cramps* aren't allowed in my class, *either*! That's *three* checks for you, Mr. Luu! No final recess!"

Daisy gargled.

"O-okay," Owen said. He slowly brought his leg back under his desk, pressing the note down hard into the carpet.

"*Now,*" Mr. St. Cupid said. He returned to the front of the classroom. "If I had *five* onions, and I ate *three*, what would— *Mister* Luu!" He pointed to Owen's foot. "Is that a *note*?"

Daisy sucked in all her breath and puffed out her cheeks.

Owen's face was red as a rib of rhubarb. "M-maybe?" he said.

"Hand it over!"

Daisy crossed her fingers.

Owen scooped the note off the floor. "I didn't, um, write it," he said as he gave it to the teacher.

Daisy crossed her toes.

"I d-don't even know what it, um, says."

Daisy crossed her eyes.

"*Well,*" Mr. St. Cupid said, "why don't we all find out *together* then?" And he unfolded the paper and began to read aloud.

If Mr. St. Upid ate three onions, he'd be left with stinky breath.

"Class!" Mr. St. Cupid hollered. "Whoever wrote this *note* has broken a very serious *rule*."

Daisy's eyeballs were bulging from holding her breath too long.

"My *name*," Mr. St. Cupid said, "is spelled like *this*."

He wrote it on the board.

MR. ST. CUPID

"It has a *C* in it, class. St. *Cupid*. Not St. *Upid*." He wrote that on the board, too.

MR. ST. UPID

"I simply *cannot* understand why my students continue to spell my name incorrectly *every* year. *Rule number thirty-nine!*" He pointed to the list:

No spelling anything rong

"*Now!*" Mr. St. Cupid shouted. "Let us *return* to *math!*"

Daisy returned to breathing.

"If I had *five*—"

Mr. St. Cupid stopped talking again as he passed in front of Daisy's row. "*What* are you doing?" he bellowed.

He was looking directly at Daisy.

Daisy knocked three erasers out of her desk, which was against Rule number 77:

No dropping three things at once

But Mr. St. Cupid didn't notice.

"*Miss* Simon!" he hollered.

He wasn't hollering at Daisy.

He was hollering at Sophie Simon.

The teacher strode over to Sophie's desk. "*Miss* Simon!" he shouted, spitting a little on the *s*'s. "Are you reading a *book* under your *desk* during *math* time?"

Sophie Simon always read books under her desk during math time. Daisy had been watching her do it all year. Sophie read books under her desk during science time, too. And during language arts time, and social studies time, and music time.

During silent reading time, she worked on chemistry experiments.

Sophie placed a finger in her book and looked up at Mr. St. Cupid. She showed him what she was reading.

"*Principles of Civil Disobedience,*" he read.

"Yes," Sophie said. "It's all about how, throughout history, people who were *absolutely powerless*"— Daisy's ears perked up—"fought against authority by refusing to follow laws or rules they felt were *utterly unfair.*" Daisy sat up a little straighter in her desk. "Like in India in 1930," Sophie went on, "when the government made buying salt illegal so a man named Gandhi led a march to the seashore to collect it. And in North Carolina in 1960, when African-Americans weren't served at lunch counters because of their race, so they staged protests called 'sit-ins.' Or nowadays, when parents won't buy their children graphing calculators, so the kids have to figure out how—"

Mr. St. Cupid slapped a hand on Sophie's desk.

"Rule number sixty!" he shouted, pointing to the wall.

No reading books fatter than your head

"You will learn about *history* in *high* school!" Mr. St. Cupid bellowed at Sophie, plucking the book from her hands. *"Third* grade is for learning *subtraction* and tying your *shoes!"*

"But I already know those things," Sophie said with a sigh.

"Rule number forty-five!" Mr. St. Cupid screeched at her. He pointed.

No sighing

"*Three checks!* No final recess for *you*, Miss Simon!"

And he tossed Sophie's book in the garbage can.

As Mr. St. Cupid went back to hollering about onions, Daisy sat at her desk and thought.

Was it really true that powerless people could find a way to change their lives, like Sophie had said? Just by refusing to do something they didn't think was fair?

Was all of that in the book Sophie had been reading?

Daisy stared at the garbage can.

Maybe, she thought, there was some hope for her after all.

"Miss Pete!"

Daisy looked up to see Mr. St. Cupid glaring down at her. His cheeks were puffed out like tomatoes.

"Why aren't you paying *attention*?"

Daisy blinked. "I was just . . ." she said, "thinking."

"Unacceptable!" Mr. St. Cupid shouted. "New rule!"

And he walked over to his list of rules and added a new one.

Then he put a third check mark by Daisy's name.

While everyone else was outside for final recess, Daisy and Owen were cleaning windows with squeegees.

Sophie was not cleaning windows with a squeegee.

She was reading her book from the garbage can.

"Sophie?" Daisy said.

Sophie did not look up.

Daisy tried again. "Can you help me with something?"

"No, thank you," Sophie said, turning a page. "I'd rather not."

Daisy looked over at Owen, but he was busy squeegeeing his window.

"I need your help," Daisy told Sophie. "I need you to teach me about that civil disinfectant stuff."

"Civil disobedience?" Sophie said.

"Yeah." Daisy nodded. "I need to learn how to get out of my ballet recital tomorrow. Does it say anything about that in there?" She pointed to the book.

"No," Sophie said.

She turned another page.

"Look," Daisy told her, waving her squeegee in the air. "Haven't you ever had a problem of your own?"

A blob of water flew off the squeegee and landed—*PLOP!*—at Sophie's feet.

Sophie kept reading.

"A really really *big* problem?" Daisy went on.

Another two blobs flew off the squeegee and landed—*PLOP! PLOP!*—on Sophie's head.

Sophie still kept reading.

"A problem so huge," Daisy said, "that you thought there'd never be any way to solve it?"

Three more blobs landed—*PLOP! PLOP! PLOP!*—right in the middle of Sophie's book.

Sophie Simon finally raised her head.

"I want a calculator," she said. "A Pembo Q-60. It's the very latest model. It costs one hundred dollars."

Daisy thought that one hundred dollars sounded like an awful lot of money for a calculator. But she didn't say that.

"I can help you get it," she said instead. "If you get me out of my ballet recital."

Sophie raised her eyebrows. "Do you have one hundred dollars?"

"No," Daisy said. "I only have"—she added up all her saved allowance—"five. But I bet the other girls in my ballet class would chip in, too. *No one* wants to dance in the recital tomorrow. There are thirteen of us, and we could each give you five dollars. That's enough, right?"

Sophie frowned at Daisy.

"If thirteen ballerinas each gave me five dollars," she said, "I'd only have sixty-five."

Daisy scratched her cheek. "So that's not enough then?" she asked.

"I'd still need thirty-five more dollars for my calculator."

From the window, Owen hiccuped.

"But you could help me anyway," Daisy told her.

The bell rang for the end of final recess. Owen crossed the room to put away his squeegee.

"I don't see why I should help you get out of your recital," Sophie said, "if you can't help me get a calculator."

"But—"

"Anyway," Sophie went on, "the principles of civil disobedience would never work in your case. You'd need someone from the newspaper to cover the story, and we couldn't find anyone on such short notice."

"The newspaper?" Daisy asked.

She didn't know anyone who worked for a newspaper.

Sophie shrugged. "Sorry."

And with that, she walked over to Mr. St. Cupid's desk, tucked her book back in the garbage can under a slimy banana peel, and sat down at her desk.

Daisy sighed and walked to the suds bucket to put her squeegee back.

She slipped—*SWISH!*

And tripped—*CLUNK!*

And crashed—*THUD!*

"Rule number twenty-nine!" Mr. St. Cupid hollered as he entered the room. *"No falling on your butt in the squeegee water!"*

This, Daisy thought as she lay on her rear end in the middle of the classroom, was exactly why she needed to get out of that recital tomorrow.

But if Sophie wouldn't help her, what could she do?

Piranhas and Pet Stores

Every afternoon, on the Number 17 bus coming home from school, Owen Luu sat in the exact same seat.

The second seat from the front, on the right side.

He always sat there with his best friend, Julia McGreevy. Julia didn't care which seat she sat in, but it was very important to Owen.

The second seat on the right was the cleanest one on the whole bus.

It didn't have dirt smears on the seat.

It didn't have stuffing coming out of the bench.

It didn't have gum underneath that your leg might stick to.

Owen hated dirty bus seats. They were grimy and messy and gross. Owen didn't like being grimy and messy and gross. He was happiest when his clothes were ironed, his ears were washed, and his shoelaces were double-knotted.

But on Friday afternoon, as the bus pulled away from Eisenberg Elementary, Owen wasn't sitting in his usual seat with Julia.

He was sitting in the fourth seat from the back on the left side, which was the second to grossest seat on the whole bus.

And he was sitting next to Sophie Simon.

Owen was sitting there because he had a problem.

A huge problem.

An *enormous* problem.

And he was positive that Sophie Simon was the only person who could help him.

But Sophie wasn't paying any attention to him. Owen didn't even think she knew he was there. She was busy reading a gigantic book called *Basics of Human Psychology.*

Owen didn't know how Sophie could read a

book like that. He got bored halfway through the title.

Sophie sure was weird, he thought. She was always reading boring books. And talking to Sophie made his brain dizzier than a windup monkey toy.

No wonder she didn't have any friends.

Owen looked to the front of the bus. He half-hoped Julia would be looking his way so he could make "I really can't do this" eyes at her, and she'd understand and make "It's okay, come sit up here with me" eyes at him.

Julia wasn't looking his way.

She was holding a piece of paper over her head. She'd ripped one out of her green journalist's notebook and scribbled a note on it. Owen knew she'd written it just for him.

Get on with it already.

Owen ran his hands over the creases in his pants.

He turned back to Sophie Simon.

"Um, Sophie?" he said softly.

Sophie did not look up.

Owen cleared his throat and tried again.

"Um? *Sophie?*"

She still did not look up.

Maybe it was useless, Owen thought. His problem was too big. Probably even someone as smart as Sophie Simon couldn't solve a problem as big as his.

It all had to do with his birthday on Sunday.

For most kids, birthdays were happy times.

For most kids, birthdays meant pin the tail on the donkey and balloons and maybe a dinosaur cake.

Most kids did not have Owen's mother.

This year, Owen's mother was planning a "birthday pool-party extravaganza."

There would be an eight-layer ice cream cake.

There would be a high-dive contest.

And there would be an "old-fashioned taffy pull."

Owen didn't like eight-layer ice cream cakes. One of the layers always toppled off your plate and landed in your lap and got you messy.

He didn't like high-dive contests. He was terrified of heights and petrified of diving.

And he did *not* want to participate in an old-fashioned taffy pull. Taffy was sticky and sloppy and sweet. He didn't want to pull it. He didn't want to do *anything* to it.

But the worst part of Owen's birthday was the present.

Every year, Owen asked his mom for something he really, really wanted.

And every year, she got him something completely different.

Two years ago, when Owen was turning seven,

he'd asked his mom for a new pair of shoes—black lace-up ones to go with his school pants. Owen had really wanted a pair of nice, clean, shiny black school shoes.

But Mrs. Luu hadn't gotten him nice, clean, shiny black school shoes.

Instead, she'd bought him antigravity boots.

Those boots sent Owen flying into the ceiling like a rocket, and off to the hospital with a concussion.

Last year, for Owen's eighth birthday, he'd asked for a book about robots—one with colorful pictures and fun facts about robots through the ages. Owen had really wanted a nice, small, fact-filled book about robots.

But Mrs. Luu hadn't gotten him a nice, small, fact-filled book about robots.

Instead, she'd bought him an actual, life-size robot with "realistic battle action noises" and a toy laser gun.

That robot had fired sparks at Owen for five days straight, until he finally figured out how to take out the batteries.

It seemed like no matter what Owen wanted, his mother got him the *exact opposite*.

So *this* year, Owen hadn't been so sure it was a good idea to tell his mother what he wanted. But she'd promised to get him exactly what he asked for.

Crossed her heart and everything.

So Owen told her.

He said that all he wanted in the world—the only thing he'd wanted for *years*, actually—was a rabbit. A nice, gentle, soft, quiet little rabbit of his very own.

And when Owen's mom had replied, "Oh, a pet is a *fabulous* idea!" well, for a second there, Owen had thought he might actually get a birthday present he wanted for a change.

But fifteen minutes later, Owen overheard his mom on the phone with Petes' Pet Store, asking Mr. and Mrs. Pete if they had any "really exotic" pets she could buy for her son's birthday.

"Do you have any alligators or duck-billed platypuses?" she asked them. "Or maybe an aquarium full of piranhas? Owen would love that!"

Owen would *not* love an aquarium full of piranhas.

He wanted a rabbit.

But no matter how many times he told his mother that, he simply couldn't *convince* her.

She had already paid Mr. and Mrs. Pete a one-hundred-dollar deposit to find something "absolutely wild." And his birthday was in just two days. If he didn't do something quick, he'd never get a rabbit.

Sometimes Owen wondered if maybe his mother wasn't really his mother. Maybe, Owen thought, the person he *believed* was his mother was really his mom's evil twin, Esmeralda, a crazy woman who loved all the things Owen hated, like fireworks and roller coasters and jalapeño peppers. Maybe his real mother—who was much quieter and calmer and who would *never* buy him a piranha—was locked up in a cabin somewhere right now, far off in the woods, looking for a way out so she could give Owen a rabbit for his birthday.

But really, Owen knew that the woman who woke him up every morning by blaring mariachi music from the stereo *was* his real mother. Because Owen had asked his grandparents once, and they swore up and down there was no evil twin named Esmeralda. So Owen's mom was definitely not locked up in a far-off cabin.

Too bad.

But if anyone could think of a way to get his

mother to give him a rabbit, it was Sophie Simon. She was the smartest girl in the third grade, possibly the world.

All Owen had to do was ask her.

"UM, SOPHIE?"

Sophie finally looked up from her book.

"Yes?" she said.

Owen blinked. Sophie Simon made him ner‑

vous. Most things made Owen nervous—clowns and geese and moving sidewalks and Mr. St. Cupid, just to name a few. But Sophie Simon made Owen *very* nervous. He felt like she could rearrange his brain cells just by looking at him.

"Um," he said again. "Could you, um, help me with something?"

"Probably," she said. "But I'd rather not."

And she went back to reading.

"Oh."

If Sophie didn't want to help him, what was Owen supposed to do?

Owen looked toward the front of the bus again.

Julia was holding up another piece of paper.

JUST ASK HER, YOU BABY!

"Um, Sophie?" Owen said, trying to be brave. "I need your help. I want a rabbit for my birthday, but my mom wants to get me a piranha or something. She already ordered a pet from Daisy Pete's parents' store, but I don't know what it is yet. Something terrible." He bit his lip. "I really think you should help me."

Sophie turned a page. "And why should I do that?" she asked.

"Well . . ." Owen thought hard. "During final recess today you told Daisy you wanted to buy a computer."

"A calculator," Sophie corrected him. "The Pembo Q-60. The latest model."

"Right," Owen said. "And you said you'd help Daisy with her problem if she could pay you enough money."

"But she couldn't," Sophie said. "She was short thirty-five dollars."

Owen didn't see what being short had to do with anything. But he said, "Well, if you helped me, I'd give you all my birthday money from Grandpa Ricky."

Sophie looked up.

"Twenty dollars," Owen told her.

Sophie looked back down.

"That still wouldn't be enough for the calculator," she said. "Even if I helped both of you. Which is a lot of helping. I'd still need fifteen dollars."

"But—"

"What makes you think I'd be able to help you anyway?" Sophie asked him.

"Oh, I'm sure it wouldn't be too tough for someone like you to figure out!" Owen said. "You know everything. You're always reading those big, fat books."

Owen looked at the page Sophie was reading.

"Reverse Psychology," it said at the top.

"What's reverse psychology?" he asked Sophie.

Sophie stuck a finger in her book to hold her place. "It's a way to *convince* someone of one thing"—Owen's ears perked up—"by telling them you want the *exact opposite*." Owen sat up a little straighter in his seat. "Like if a teacher wanted her students to do their spelling homework, so she told them that she didn't think they could do it because they weren't smart enough. Then they would try very hard and finish their homework, just to prove her wrong. Which was exactly what she wanted in the first place."

Owen thought about that.

"Does it work on moms?" he asked.

"What?" Sophie said.

"All that stuff you just said. Reverse photography."

"Reverse psychology," Sophie corrected.

"Yeah, that one."

The bus screeched to a stop.

"Stanford Avenue!" the bus driver called out.

"Sorry," Sophie said, zipping her book into her backpack. "This is my stop."

"But—"

"I have to get off," Sophie said. She poked him in the knee. "Please move."

"But I need your help!"

Sophie sighed. "Why don't you get your friend to help you?" she asked. "That curly-haired girl. Maybe she has some ideas."

The bus doors squeaked open.

The driver went outside to direct traffic.

"Julia won't help me," Owen said as Sophie squeezed past him into the aisle. "She's too busy trying to think of a story to write for the school newspaper."

"Newspaper?"

Sophie sat down so quickly that she landed right on top of Owen.

She didn't move.

She just stared at the top of Owen's head.

"Um, Sophie?" he said. She was acting sort of weird.

Plus she was wrinkling his pants.

"Sophie?" Owen said again.

Sophie blinked at him. "Did you say that Julia is looking for a news story?"

"Yeah," Owen said. "For the school paper. But she only has until Monday, and she'll never find one. Plus she doesn't have anything to type on. Last weekend her dad made her sell her typewriter at their yard sale. She got fifteen bucks for it."

Sophie's eyes grew wide as watermelons.

"Fifteen dollars?" she asked.

"Yeah," Owen said. "Why?"

The bus driver popped his head back inside the bus.

"Anyone else for Stanford Avenue?" he shouted.

Sophie grabbed Owen's hand.

"Come on!" she hollered.

She dragged him down the bus aisle.

"But-but . . ." Owen stuttered. "Where are we going? This isn't my stop. What if I—?"

One step from the bottom, Sophie whirled around to face him. "Do you want a rabbit?" she asked him. "Or do you want a piranha?"

And she leaped down the last step to Stanford Avenue.

Owen turned to look at Julia.

She was grinning at him.

"Well?" she said. "What are you waiting for?"

And just like that, right as the doors were about to close, Owen Luu made a decision.

"Sophie, wait!" he called, throwing himself from the bus just as the doors snapped shut behind him. "Wait, Sophie, wait! I DON'T WANT A PIRANHA!"

They'd been walking for about five minutes when suddenly Sophie stopped.

"Here we are!" she cried.

They were standing in front of Petes' Pet Store.

"Wh-what are we doing here?" Owen asked. Pet stores made him nervous. They were filled with guppies and geckos and gerbils.

"You said your mom is buying your birthday present from this pet store, right?"

"R-right," Owen said.

He peeked through the window.

Daisy Pete was in there, practicing her twirling.

She was not a very good twirler.

She twirled once.

She twirled twice.

She twirled three ti—

CRASH!

Daisy fell over.

From somewhere inside the store, a parrot squawked.

"If you want to use reverse psychology on your mother"—Sophie scanned the flyers pasted in the window—"and what you really want for your birthday is a rabbit"—she ran her finger down an advertisement for pet food—"then we need to make sure that the Petes sell your mom the exact *opposite* of a rabbit."

"Okay," Owen said. "But what's the exact opposite of a rabbit?"

"Well," Sophie said. She began to read a new flyer. "Would you say that a rabbit has long ears?"

Owen stuck his hands in his pockets. "Of course," he said.

"And would you say that it has a short, fluffy tail?"

"Very short," Owen told her. "And fluffy."

"And would you also say," Sophie went on, running her finger over the last row of flyers, "that a rabbit is very, very quiet?"

Owen nodded. "So the opposite of a rabbit," he said, beginning to understand, "would have short ears, a long tail, and be very, very loud?"

Sophie didn't answer him.

Instead, she slapped her hand over a flyer in the window.

"Perfect!" she cried out.

Owen squinted at the flyer.

When he turned back to talk to Sophie, she was inside the pet store.

Owen stood outside, staring at the flyer in the window. And he was still standing there two minutes later when Sophie popped her blond head out the door.

"Owen, come on!" she called to him. "Come on in here! We need to talk to Daisy. Oh, and you can get a letter to Julia for me, right?"

"Huh?"

But Sophie had disappeared inside the store again.

Owen gulped as he opened the door to the pet store.

Sophie Simon *and* pets?

What had he gotten himself into?

Very Ugly Hats

Julia McGreevy parked her bike in front of the Middlebury Performing Arts Center and looked up at the marquee.

Madame Robespierre
In Association with Eisenberg Elementary
Presents:
OOH LA LA
A ballet recital about the history of France

Blech, Julia thought.
Julia did not like ballet recitals.

She thought they were boring.

And long.

And pink.

But last night Julia had found a note slipped under her front door, a note that made her want to come to this particular ballet recital very badly.

Julia,

> *Looking for a big scoop?*
> *Middlebury P.A.C. 2:00 p.m. tomorrow.*
> *Bring fifteen dollars and your camera. Come in the rear entrance, and don't let anyone see you.*
>
> *You won't be disappointed.*
>
> *—Sophie Simon*
>
> *P.S. Owen says hi.*

Julia pulled her camera out of her bike basket and hung it around her neck.

She patted the folded bills in her pocket.

She checked her watch.

1:52.

Right on time.

Julia slipped inside the back door, which was propped open with a brick.

Julia sneaked past the dressing rooms, where

girls were busy getting ready. She didn't see Sophie Simon anywhere. How was Julia supposed to figure out what the big news story was if Sophie wasn't there to tell her? What a weirdo. All that girl ever did was read about boring stuff like history. And talking to her always made Julia feel like she was in the middle of a one-kid brain tornado.

No wonder she didn't have any friends.

Still, if Sophie could find Julia a big news story, it was definitely worth paying her fifteen dollars.

Julia really, really needed a big news story.

Every Monday, Julia turned in a story for the weekly paper. Stories about the mysterious meat loaf in the cafeteria, or the contaminated candy machine outside the teachers' lounge.

They were pretty good stories.

But every Tuesday, Miss Harbinger told Julia that she didn't print anyone's stories unless they were in fifth grade or higher.

That was *the Rule*.

But what Miss Harbinger didn't know was that, if Julia didn't publish a story in next week's paper, her dad was going to make her drop out of the journalism club.

And then, whether Julia liked it or not—and

Julia did *not*—her dad was going to make her sign up for the Math Olympics team.

As a mathlete.

Julia was not a mathlete. She was a journalist.

She just had to get a story published to prove it.

A man burst into the hallway. He was dressed all in black and had a headset stuck over his ears. "Five minutes to curtain!" he hollered.

He ignored Julia as he rushed past.

"Everybody to the stage!"

Well, Julia thought, if everyone else was going to the stage, she should, too. That was what a good journalist would do.

Julia ducked through the stage door and hid under a prop table on the side of the stage.

No one noticed her.

It was dark. The stage lights were off and the curtain was closed. Julia could hear murmurs from the audience on the other side.

It sounded like a big crowd.

Julia took her pencil from behind her ear and scribbled a note in the notebook she always kept in her back pocket.

PACKED AT THE P.A.C.

Julia always took lots of notes when she was working on a story. A reporter couldn't risk forgetting anything. It was just being smart.

Her father wouldn't think it was smart.

Professor McGreevy thought that there wasn't anything *smart* about working on a school newspaper.

The only thing Julia's dad thought about, all day every day, was math.

Math, math, math, math, math.

He quizzed Julia on her times tables over her morning cornflakes.

He picked her up early from birthday parties to talk about long division.

He even tucked her into bed with stories about Isaac Newton.

Ever since the day she was born, Professor McGreevy had been trying to make Julia as nuts about math as he was.

It was not going to work.

Julia McGreevy hated math worse than she hated the color pink.

Sometimes Julia wondered if maybe her father wasn't really her father. Maybe, Julia thought, sometime just after she was born, her dad had been hit over the head with a very large abacus, and it had shaken up his brain so much that he'd gotten amnesia. Maybe he'd forgotten all the things he *used* to like—normal dad things like golfing and barbecues, and reading bedtime stories like *The Tale of Peter Rabbit*—and now all he could remember were math problems. Maybe, Julia thought, if she just whacked her father hard enough in the right spot, he'd go back to being the nice, normal, non-mathy dad he was before.

But really, Julia knew that her father had always been the same math nerd he was today. Because sometimes he'd say things like "Back when I was your age, my team had won the regional Math Olympics three times already," and she'd seen the photos, too. So there most definitely was no need to whack her father over the head with something heavy.

Too bad.

Behind her, Julia heard a group coming through the stage door. She poked her head out from under the table to watch and listen.

One by one, the ballerinas filed past Julia's hiding spot and lined up on the stage. From underneath the table, Julia couldn't see any of the girls' heads—just their pink tutus and pink ballet slippers.

They were followed by a tall, thin woman holding a large wooden stick.

That must be Madame Robespierre.

Pound!

Madame Robespierre banged her stick on the ground as the last ballerina lined up onstage.

Julia counted them.

Thirteen.

Thirteen tiny, terrified tots in tutus.

Pound!

"Lay-DEEZ!" Madame Robespierre hollered at them.

She had a thick French accent, with vowels as sharp as her pointy shoes.

"Tonight you are telling zee 'istory of France!"

Pound!

"Zee story of my country!"

Pound!

"So you will wear zee 'atts proud-lee and zere will be no complaining!"

Pound!

Julia pulled her pencil out from behind her ear and scribbled in her notebook.

ATTS? she wrote. What was an att?

Julia inched out of her hiding spot to see.

She sucked in a breath when she saw what the girls had on their heads.

She had never seen anything so ugly.

HATS, Julia wrote in her notebook. *VERY UGLY HATS.*

Each one of the very ugly hats, which were also very large, was shaped like a different object, and

58

Julia guessed that they must all have something to do with France.

One girl was balancing an enormous wedge of stinky cheese, while another girl was teetering underneath a hat shaped like a huge bottle of perfume. A brown-haired girl across the stage was strapped to what appeared to be a two-ton plate of frogs' legs.

But the biggest and ugliest hat of all was Daisy Pete's. It was a gigantic sculpture, at least two feet high, that Julia recognized as an exact replica of the Eiffel Tower.

Julia thought that if she had to wear a humongous hat like that, she would topple over in a millisecond.

Was *this* why Sophie had told her to come today? Julia wondered. To see the giant ugly hats?

Pound!

Madame Robespierre slammed her stick on the ground again.

Pound!

"Zere will be absolutely no steenk-ing tonight," she hollered. "Do we all understand zat?"

Madame looked down her nose at each girl in turn.

Pound!

"Because sometimes you all steenk quite bad-lee!"

Julia wrote a new note in her book.

MRS. R. = NOT NICE

Pound!
Daisy Pete raised a hand.
Pound!
"What eez it, you stu-peed girl?" Madame asked.

In her notebook, Julia crossed out *NOT NICE* and wrote *MEAN*.

"Um, well," Daisy said. "I was just wondering, um, what if I *do* fall over? What if I . . . lose my balance?"

The other girls gasped.

Julia leaned forward until her neck was stretched like a rubber band.

Madame Robespierre did not pound her stick. She didn't shout.

She didn't do any of the things that Julia thought she might.

Instead, she straightened her back and looked down at Daisy with a calm smile.

"It is very important to have zee balance," she said.

Daisy nodded.

"But zee problem," Madame said, "it is zee little baby toes."

She scratched her chin.

"Zey are no good for zee balance."

Madame Robespierre leaned down close, until her nose was just an inch away from Daisy's.

Daisy was shaking. The tower on her head looked like it was in the middle of an earthquake.

"So," Madame continued, "zee ballerinas in Par-ee"—Julia knew that this was the weird French way of saying *Paris*—"do you know what zey do to keep zee balance? Do you know what zey do with zese stu-peed baby toes?"

Daisy shook her head, her eyes as big as volleyballs.

Pound!

"ZEY CHOP ZEM OFF!" Madame Robespierre hollered.

Pound!

"*ZAT* IS WHAT ZEY DO TO ZEE BABY TOES!"

Pound pound!

"Any girl who falls oh-verrrr tonight," Madame screeched, "we will chop off zer toes!"

And just like that, she marched off the stage, her heels clackity-clickity-clackity-clicking.

Julia crossed out *MEAN* in her notebook and drew a picture of the Wicked Witch of the West.

On the other side of the curtain, the orchestra began to play. The ballerinas scrambled to their places.

Julia was worried.

What if Daisy really did fall over?

What if Madame Robespierre really did chop off her baby toes?

Was that why Sophie had asked Julia to come? Was that the big scoop she'd been talking about?

Just before the curtain rose, Julia noticed something across the stage. On the side opposite her, crouching under a folding table just like she was, there was a small, blond person.

Not just any small, blond person.

Sophie Simon.

Sophie was reading a book.

The curtain went up, and the audience cheered. The lights were bright and the music was loud.

Julia could see Daisy's parents in the very first row.

The ballerinas began to twirl, their giant, ugly hats spinning above them.

They twirled once.

They twirled twice.

Three times they twirled.

And four.

And five.

Daisy, so far, had not fallen over.

Julia wanted to write *LOTS OF TWIRLING* in her notebook, but she was too busy staring at Daisy.

On the one hand, Julia *really really* did NOT want Daisy to fall over. If Daisy fell over, she was going to be two toes short of a full set. And that would be a very bad thing.

On the other hand, Julia *really really* DID want Daisy to fall over. If Daisy fell over, there would definitely be something newsworthy to write about. And that would be a very good thing.

This, Julia thought, was what Miss Harbinger would call "a reporter's dilemma."

As she finished the tenth twirl, Daisy Pete began to look queasy.

On the fifteenth twirl, her face was as green as a toad's.

On the seventeenth twirl, the tip of the tower on top of her hat began to wobble.

On the eighteenth twirl, it wibbled.

And on the nineteenth twirl, in front of Madame Robespierre and her parents and everyone, Daisy Pete fell right smack on the ground.

The hat tumbled off her head and onto the stage.

The Eiffel Tower broke in half.

Julia gasped.

The audience gasped.

The *ballerinas* gasped.

The orchestra stopped playing, and the girls onstage stopped dancing.

Daisy Pete looked like she was going to cry.

Everyone was waiting—waiting, waiting, *waiting*—to see what would happen.

But just as Madame Robespierre leaped out of her seat—to chop off Daisy's baby toes, or possibly worse—Julia heard a holler from the other side of the stage.

"Remember what I told you!" the voice bellowed.

It was Sophie Simon, her fists balled up at her waist.

All of the ballerinas turned to look at her.

"Remember!" she shouted to them. "Fight for what's right! Just follow Daisy!"

And just like that, every single one of the ballerinas hiked up her tutu and sat down on the stage to join Daisy where she lay in a crumbled heap.

Madame Robespierre bounded up the stage steps two at a time.

She did not look pleased.

"WHAT IS GO-ING ON?" she hollered at her dancers.

Daisy sat up slowly. She looked at Madame Robespierre, and for the first time all night, Julia thought she didn't look afraid.

Julia placed her pencil over her notebook and got ready.

Something important was about to happen, she just knew it.

Daisy smiled at Madame Robespierre, a slow stretch of a smile that showed all her teeth.

"Madame Robespierre," Daisy said. "We're not going to dance anymore. Not until your"—Daisy glanced over at Sophie—"until your tyrannical domination over this dance company has ceased."

The audience began to murmur, and Julia did
her best to spell *TYRANNICAL DOMINATION*
in her notebook.

Madame Robespierre glared at Daisy.

"What is zese joke?" she hissed at her.

"It's not a joke," Daisy said, firmer this time.
"We're staging a sit-in."

The other girls nodded.

"By sitting on the stage."

"A SEET-IN!" Madame hollered. *Pound!* "Ballerinas do not seet!" *Pound!* "Zey dance!"

Madame shouted at the orchestra to start playing again. But even as the music swelled around them, the ballerinas refused to dance.

They just sat.

Julia could see the people in the audience shaking their heads and whispering to each other.

"DANCE!" Madame screeched. She tried to lift Daisy to her feet, but Daisy's body hung like a limp noodle, and she refused to stand up.

Madame tried to lift the other girls, but they made their bodies limp, too.

They didn't look much like ballerinas, Julia thought.

They looked more like boiled broccoli.

Not one of the dancers was going to dance.

Now this, Julia thought, was a news story.

Julia set down her notebook and picked up her camera. As Madame pounded her stick on the ground, trying to haul her dancers to their feet at the same time, Julia clicked photographs.

Click!

Pound!

Click!

Pound!

Click click click!

POUND!

"YOU ARE ZEE BALLERINAS!" Madame Robespierre bellowed. Her hair was flying from her bun in frightening wisps. "YOU WILL *DANCE!*"

Julia took another photo.

One by one, parents rose from their seats and climbed to the stage to scoop their pink-tutued daughters into their arms and walk out of the theater.

And as they exited the stage, Julia noticed that each girl handed Sophie Simon what appeared to be a five-dollar bill.

By the time Mr. and Mrs. Pete got to the stage, Daisy was the last ballerina left.

"Madame Robespierre," Mr. Pete said. "I think I speak for everyone in this town when I say that my daughter will *not* be attending your school of dance ever again. I'll be talking to the school board immediately and asking for your resignation. Your days in this business are over."

He turned to Daisy then, and held out a hand for her.

Daisy slowly rose to her feet.

She bent carefully at the waist.

She took a long, deep bow.

The audience went wild with applause.

Julia couldn't help but smile as Madame Robespierre ran off the stage.

She knew for a fact that her story was going to make the paper this time. She even had the perfect headline.

ROBESPIERRE GETS THE AX.

Now, she thought, if only she could figure out a way for her best friend, Owen, to get that rabbit he'd been wanting for his birthday . . .

The Lemur at the
Pool Party

Sophie's parents often drove Sophie bananas.

But they had never driven Sophie more bananas than on that Sunday afternoon, as they dropped her off at Owen Luu's birthday party.

"Oh, dill pickle!" Sophie's mother gushed as they walked into the backyard. Kids were already swimming and splashing in the pool. The girls were wearing bathing suits, and the boys were wearing swim trunks. Everyone was giggling and happy and looked thrilled to be at a birthday pool party.

Everyone, that is, except Owen and Sophie.

Owen was wearing green dolphin trunks with a dress shirt and tie.

Sophie had cargo pants on over her swimsuit, and her pockets were stuffed with objects she'd sneaked from home.

Very, very strange objects.

Objects she thought might come in handy.

"Oh, isn't this exciting, jelly bean?" Sophie's mother went on. "You're going to have so much fun!"

Sophie rolled her eyes to the right. She had *not* come to the party to have fun.

"Yes, biscuit!" Sophie's father exclaimed. "I think this will be the perfect place for you to make some friends!"

Sophie rolled her eyes to the left. She had *not* come to the party to make friends.

Sophie Simon had come to the birthday party to make sure Owen got his rabbit.

Then he would give her twenty dollars, and Sophie could finally buy the graphing calculator of her dreams.

The Pembo Q-60.

The latest model.

She turned to her parents.

"Mom?" she said. "Dad? Can you guys leave now?"

"Oh, Maxwell," Sophie's mother said to her

71

husband. "Did you hear that? Our little pudding pop wants nothing to do with us." She wiped away a tear. "Isn't that *wonderful*?"

Sophie's father nodded. "She's pushing away her caretakers," he said. "Just like Doctor Wanda was talking about last Wednesday."

"Our little banana cream pie is finally becoming well-adjusted."

"Mom?" Sophie said. "Dad? Seriously, will you leave?"

"Of course, my darling little lettuce wedge," her father said. "Here." He handed Sophie a sparkly blue gift bag. "Don't forget Owen's present. I hope he likes what you picked out."

"Mmm-hmm," Sophie said.

She wasn't listening.

She was looking around for Daisy.

"Goodbye, my apple crumble!" her mother said, kissing her on the left cheek.

"Have fun, wonton!" her father said, kissing her on the right cheek.

Sophie waited for her parents to leave, and then she wiped off both her cheeks. An "apple crumble" plus a "wonton" was enough to make her seriously ill.

Sophie spotted Daisy by the present table. She

was leaning over a wooden crate, making chirping noises.

Either Daisy had lost her mind, Sophie thought, or inside that crate was a ring-tailed lemur.

She went over to see which it was.

"Hi, Sophie!" Daisy called to her. "Do you want to meet Lenny the Lemur?"

Sophie bent down and peeked through the slats of the crate.

Staring back at her was a ring-tailed lemur. It looked just like the one Sophie had seen in the flyer outside the pet store.

The lemur had very short ears.

The lemur had a long, bushy tail.

"Yap!"

The lemur had a very noisy yap.

"Perfect," Sophie said.

Lenny the Lemur was the exact opposite of a rabbit.

"Where did you get him?" she asked Daisy.

Daisy poked a finger through the crate to rub Lenny's fur. "My cousin Matilda runs a rescue center for exotic animals. She's letting me borrow him for the day."

Sophie nodded. "And Mrs. Luu thinks this is the pet your parents picked for Owen?"

"Yep," Daisy said.

"Yap!" Lenny yapped.

"And your parents don't suspect anything?"

"Nope," Daisy said. "I told them Owen's mom called and said she changed her mind."

"Yap!" Lenny yapped.

"I think," Sophie said, "that everything will work out perfectly."

When all of the guests had arrived, Mrs. Luu told them they were going to open presents first.

Owen began to unwrap his gifts. Everyone crowded around him to see what presents he got.

Everyone, that is, except Sophie.

Sophie didn't care what presents Owen got. Unless he unwrapped a graphing calculator, she wasn't interested.

Owen did not unwrap a graphing calculator.

He unwrapped board games and card games and video games and loads of other stuff that Sophie found extremely boring.

From Julia, he got a box of rabbit food.

From Daisy, he got a rabbit cage.

From Sophie, he got an empty blue bag.

Owen turned the bag upside down.

"Where's my present?" he asked.

"Oh," Sophie said. "I guess I forgot to put it in there. But you can keep the bag if you want."

"Um, thanks," Owen said.

"You're welcome," Sophie told him.

Mrs. Luu clapped her hands together. "And now, Owen," she said, "it's time to give you *my* present."

She pulled the crate out from under the table.

She pried off the lid.

Inside was Lenny the Lemur.

At last, Sophie thought. *Now* things were getting interesting.

Lenny leaped out of the crate and scrambled onto Owen's shoulder, cuddling in the nook by his neck.

Owen looked like he'd rather spend an hour on the tilt-a-whirl after drinking a barrel of pickle juice than be snuggled around the neck by a ringtailed lemur.

"Isn't he *fantastic*, Owen?" Mrs. Luu cried. "It's exactly what you wanted!"

"I-I . . . It's . . . I . . ." Lenny was licking his claws and staring at Owen. Owen gulped. "It-it . . . I . . ."

Sophie poked him in the side.

"It's perfect," Owen said. He gulped again. "It's exactly the exact same pet I wanted. Exactly."

"I knew you would love it!" Mrs. Luu exclaimed. "Now! Time for cake!"

While Mrs. Luu lit the candles, Sophie thought about the most recent book she'd checked out from the library.

Fascinating Facts About Ring-Tailed Lemurs

She thought about one chapter in particular.

"The Diet of the Ring-Tailed Lemur"

There were lots of interesting bits of information in that chapter, but there was one fact that Sophie had found *especially* fascinating:

One of a lemur's favorite snacks is grasshoppers.

Mrs. Luu finished lighting the candles.

Sophie scooched to the very back of the crowd of kids, far away from Mrs. Luu.

"Everybody sing!" Mrs. Luu called out.

"Happy birthday to you!" they all sang.

Sophie reached inside her right pocket.

"Happy birthday to you!"

She pulled out a handful of grasshoppers she'd found in her yard.

"Happy birthday, dear Owen!"

She tossed the grasshoppers up in the air, and they landed—*plunk plunk plunk plunk*—right on top of the cake.

"Happy bir—"

"YAP!"

Lenny the Lemur leaped from Owen's shoulder and pounced onto the cake, trying to grab the grasshoppers.

He snuffed out the candles.

"Yap!"

The cake toppled over.

"Yap!"

Fur and frosting went flying.

"Yap!"

"Owen, your birthday cake!" Mrs. Luu screamed. She yanked Lenny out of the frosting and dropped him on the grass. "I spent seventeen hours perfecting the icing! And now it's *ruined*!"

Sophie smiled.

"Th-that's okay, Mom," Owen said slowly. "I

don't mind. That lemur is the exact pet I exactly wanted. Exactly."

Mrs. Luu sniffed. "Well," she said, examining the frosted, ice creamy lemur at her feet. "Okay then. I'm glad you're so happy. I guess it's time for the high-dive contest."

While Mrs. Luu led the children to the diving board, Sophie scooped up Lenny the Lemur and set him on her shoulder.

Lenny licked his cakey claws, and Sophie winked at him.

Sophie thought about another chapter in the book about lemurs.

"The Social Habits of the Ring-Tailed Lemur"

There were tons of exciting pieces of information in that chapter, but there was one fact that Sophie had found *especially* remarkable:

When lemurs get cold, they like to warm their bellies in the sun. They can stay perfectly still for hours.

Mrs. Luu snapped her fingers. "Everybody in line for the diving board!" she cried.

Everyone lined up behind the diving board ladder.

Sophie stood at the back of the line, Lenny perched on her shoulder.

She reached inside her left pocket.

She pulled out the battery-powered fan she'd brought from home.

She turned the fan on high and shot the frosty air at the ice-cream-covered lemur.

"YAP!"

Lenny leaped from her shoulder and raced up the ladder.

He plopped himself down—*PLOP!*—in the sunny spot at the very center of the diving board.

"Oh no!" Mrs. Luu shouted, staring up at the lemur high above the pool. He had his belly to the sun, his little lemur arms out to the sides. "How can we have a high-dive contest when there's a *lemur* on the diving board?"

Owen shrugged.

He did not seem very upset about not being able to dive.

Mrs. Luu stomped to the front of the line and climbed the ladder.

She walked to the edge, one wobbly footstep at a time.

She tried to pry Lenny off the diving board.

She poked and prodded.

"*Yap!*"

The diving board flopped, and Mrs. Luu bounced. Down below, the kids held their breath. But Mrs. Luu kept her balance and did not fall into the pool.

She tugged and tickled.

"Yap!"

The diving board flipped, and Mrs. Luu bobbed. Down below, the kids held their breath. But Mrs. Luu kept her balance and did not fall into the pool.

She jerked and jostled.

"YAP!"

The diving board flip–flip–flop–flop–flipped, and Mrs. Luu bumped and bopped and bucked. Down below, the kids held their breath. But Mrs. Luu kept her balance.

She did not fall into the pool.

And that lemur would not move a muscle.

"I had this diving board installed especially for your birthday extravaganza!" Mrs. Luu wailed across the water. "And now the high-dive contest is *ruined*!"

Sophie smiled.

"I-I don't mind, Mom," Owen said. "Really. I still exactly love that exact lemur exactly up there."

"Well," she said once she had climbed down the ladder. "As long as you're happy, Owen." She looked up at Lenny and shook her head. "I guess it's time for the old-fashioned taffy pull."

While Mrs. Luu set out the pot of taffy mixture on the table, Sophie thought about Chapter 3 in the book about lemurs.

"Predators of the Ring-Tailed Lemur"

There were loads of incredible nuggets of information in that chapter, but there was one fact that Sophie had found *especially* amazing.

One of a lemur's fiercest enemies is the Madagascar ground boa. If confronted with a boa constrictor, a lemur will attack.

Mrs. Luu pointed to the pot of syrupy taffy mixture. "Who wants to add the food coloring?" she asked.

Sophie looked at the bottles of food coloring.
She picked up a bottle labeled "Jungle Green."
"I'll do it," she said.
She unscrewed the lid.
"Just a tiny titch," Mrs. Luu told her.
Sophie nodded.
She poured in a tiny titch.
Then she poured in the tiniest titch more.
"That's enough," Mrs. Luu told her.

"Okay," Sophie said.

She grinned at Owen.

And then she poured in the whole bottle.

"Whoops," she said. "It must have slipped."

Mrs. Luu took the bottle from Sophie and frowned at her.

"Now," Mrs. Luu told the children after she had stirred in the dye, "in order to turn this mixture into candy, we have to pull it. I'll show you. You just grab a great glob like this"—Mrs. Luu reached in the pot—"and then you take it in both your hands"—she took hold of a heaping blob of dark green goop—"and you stretch it."

Mrs. Luu began to pull.

Slowly . . .

Slowly . . .

Longer . . .

And longer . . .

Until the taffy between her hands looked exactly like one long, thin, green—

"Yap!"

—snake.

"Yap yap!"

A Madagascar ground boa, to be exact.

"Yap yap yap!"

From up on his high-dive perch, Lenny had spotted the taffy.

"What on earth," Mrs. Luu said, the taffy stretched out between her hands, "is that lemur yapping abou—"

"YAP!"

That's when she was kicked in the taffy by a high-diving lemur.

"YAP!"

Lenny scuffled with the taffy, and Mrs. Luu knocked over the taffy pot.

CRASH!

"YAP!"

Mrs. Luu hollered.

Lenny tussled with the taffy, and Mrs. Luu toppled onto the table.

BASH!

"YAP!"

Mrs. Luu screamed.

Lenny wrestled with the taffy, and Mrs. Luu, her feet just inches from the edge of the pool . . .

Lost her balance . . .

And tumbled into the water.

SPLASH!

"YAP!"

Mrs. Luu wailed.

"That's it!" Mrs. Luu screeched from the water. She climbed out of the pool.

Her dress was soaked.

Her shoe was broken.

Her hair was stuck to her eyebrows.

The taffy was toast.

"I tried out twenty-two different recipes to make that taffy!" Mrs. Luu bellowed. "And that lemur *ruined* it! He ruined *everything!*"

Sophie smiled.

"But I *love* the lemur," Owen said. He scooped Lenny out of the pool and handed him to Daisy, sticky and dripping and taffyed all over. "He's exactly the pet I wanted. Exactly."

"Well, I'm sorry, Owen," Mrs. Luu said. She wrung out her sleeves. "But I never should have agreed to get you such an exotic pet. I knew it was a mistake from the beginning."

She squeezed the water out of her hair.

"A lemur clearly isn't a good pet for you," she said. "You need something totally different. Like a rabbit. Yes. A nice, quiet rabbit with long ears and a fluffy little tail."

Owen nodded slowly. "Yeah, Mom," he said. "That doesn't sound too ba—"

"No arguments!" Mrs. Luu scolded. "You're

getting a rabbit and there's nothing you can do to change my mind!"

Owen slipped Sophie a twenty-dollar bill.

"I guess that's fine then," he told his mother.

Sophie smiled and tucked the bill in her pocket with the rest of her money.

One hundred dollars.

Sophie finally had one hundred dollars.

She had done it. She had thought of every detail and solved every problem. And now she had exactly enough money to get the Pembo Q-60.

Mrs. Luu took off her shoes and dumped out the pool water. "I'm going to call Petes' Pets right now and ask for my money back," she said.

Sophie stopped smiling.

It turned out there was *one* detail she hadn't thought of.

"What?" she asked Mrs. Luu.

"I'm going to call the pet store," Mrs. Luu said. "I paid one hundred dollars for that lemur, and I want my money back."

And she turned and walked, drippy-sticky, toward the house.

"Sophie!" Daisy hissed. "She can't call my parents! I'll get in trouble! What if they make me go back to ballet class?"

Julia's eyes were big as cantaloupes. "If Daisy goes back to ballet class," she cried, "then I won't have a news story!"

Owen sat down plop in the grass. "If my mom finds out about the lemur," he said, "she'll *never* get me a rabbit!"

Sophie stuck her hand inside her pocket.

One hundred dollars.

She looked at Daisy.

She looked at Julia.

She looked at Owen.

Sophie sighed.

"Mrs. Luu!" she called out.

Mrs. Luu turned.

"You don't need to call the pet store!" Sophie hollered.

Mrs. Luu walked back to the pool.

"Daisy has your refund," Sophie said. She took the money out of her pocket and slipped it secretly into Daisy's hand. "One hundred dollars. Her parents made her bring it in case there was a problem."

Daisy looked at the money, and then she looked at Sophie.

Sophie nodded.

Daisy handed the money to Mrs. Luu.

"Thank you," Mrs. Luu said. She walked back inside the house, leaving soggy footsteps all the way.

And then something happened to Sophie that had never happened before.

Daisy hugged her.

And Julia hugged her.

And *Owen* hugged her.

"Sophie!" Julia cried. The four of them were squeezed up tight together like a human snowball. "I think you may just be the best friend I've ever, ever had."

And Owen and Daisy agreed.

Sophie thought about that.

Somehow, Sophie had not ended up with a calculator.

Somehow, she had ended up with friends.

What on earth was she supposed to do with *those*?

If Sophie Simon had been paying attention during the rest of the party, instead of sulking behind the broken cake table with the soggy, taffy-covered lemur, she would have noticed several things.

She would have noticed Daisy whispering to Owen.

She would have noticed Owen whispering to Julia.

And she would have noticed that when Julia's father, Professor McGreevy, showed up early to talk to his daughter about long division, Julia whispered to him.

But Sophie didn't notice any of those things.

By the time Sophie's parents came to pick her up, she was miserable.

Sad.

Sullen.

Sunk.

"Hello, sweet potato!" her father greeted her. "Did you make any friends?"

"Yes," Sophie said with a sigh. "I'm afraid I did. I don't really want to talk about it."

"Oh, Maxwell," Sophie's mother said to her husband. "Did you hear that? Our little garbanzo bean is being rude and ill-mannered." She clutched her chest. "Isn't that *fabulous*?"

Sophie's father nodded. "She's refusing to talk about her personal life," he said. "Just like that well-adjusted child on Doctor Wanda's show last Thursday."

Sophie was in the middle of rolling her eyes to the right and then back again, when she heard a voice behind her.

"Excuse me."

Sophie turned around.

It was Julia's father, Professor McGreevy.

"My daughter Julia tells me there's a girl over here who's very good at math," he said. He looked at Sophie. "Would that be you?"

Sophie looked over at the pool. Owen, Daisy, and Julia were laughing and splashing each other with pool water.

"Yes," Sophie said. "I'm good at math."

"But only in a well-adjusted way," her father piped in.

"The well-adjusted amount of good," her mother added.

"Why do you want to know?" Sophie asked.

"Well," Professor McGreevy said. "Since it seems Julia won't be on the Math Olympics team this year, we're short one mathlete. And I thought you might like to join."

He turned to Sophie's parents. "It would be a great opportunity for your daughter to make friends," he told them.

"Tater Tot, did you hear that?" her mother cried. "More friends!"

Her father nodded. "Oh, lemon wedge, you could have a whole gaggle of them!"

"It's very fun," Professor McGreevy said. "Mathletically, I mean. There's a large competition, very competitive, and . . ."

Sophie stopped listening.

She did not want to join Math Olympics.

She did not want a whole gaggle of friends.

What Sophie *wanted* was a—

". . . calculator."

Sophie's head shot up.

"What did you say?" she asked Professor Mc-Greevy.

"I said," he repeated, "that each mathlete on the winning team gets a graphing calculator." Sophie's ears perked up. "The Pembo Q-60." Sophie stood a little straighter. "It's the latest model," he concluded.

Sophie looked over to the far end of the pool again.

Julia, Owen, and Daisy waved at her.

They were all grinning.

"So," Professor McGreevy said, "will you join us?"

Sophie waved back at Julia, Owen, and Daisy.

She was grinning, too.

"Sophie?" Professor McGreevy asked.

Maybe, Sophie thought, just maybe, she might actually like having friends.

"Yes," she said. "I think I might like that quite a bit."

Sophie Simon's Encyclopedia of Things She Can't Believe You Don't Know Already

antigravity boots: Boots with large springs on the bottom which allow the wearer to jump very high and far, as though he were on the moon (or on his way to the hospital).

calculus: A very difficult type of math, used to calculate volumes and formulaic changes. Most third-graders hate it more than chocolate-covered beetles.

civil disobedience: A form of protest in which people purposefully refuse to obey certain laws or rules that they feel are unfair without behaving in a violent manner. Many famous leaders, including Mahatma Gandhi and Martin Luther King, Jr., used this technique in their struggles for equal rights, and they often called in news reporters to cover the protests.

earthworm: A worm that lives in the earth. Earthworms have five "hearts," which are very different from the hearts inside humans but just as difficult to operate on.

Eiffel Tower: An iron tower in Paris, France, designed by the engineer Gustave Eiffel for the 1889 World's Fair. Over 1,000 feet tall, it stands higher than the Chrysler Building in New York City and weighs over 10,000 tons. Not a very good subject for a hat.

flan: A dessert, popular in Spain and Mexico, that is made from sugar, eggs, and milk. Sort of like pudding but wigglier.

frogs' legs: A favorite French food, often fried and served with a healthy heaping of garlic. Yum yum!

Mahatma Gandhi (1869–1948): A political and spiritual leader in India during that country's independence movement, famous for his belief in nonviolence. After the British government placed a tax on common salt—making it very difficult for many Indian citizens to pay for the necessary item—Gandhi led one of his most successful protests, the Salt March to Dandi in 1930, walking over 200 miles to the ocean in order to collect his own salt illegally.

graphing calculator: A type of calculator used to chart graphs and study calculus. Most third-graders would rather have a pony.

Greensboro sit-ins: A series of peaceful protests that helped spark the African-American civil rights movement in the United States. In February 1960, several African-American college students sat down at a "whites-only" lunch counter in a Woolworth's store in Greensboro, North Carolina, even though they knew they would not be served. After many similar protests, Woolworth's and other stores around the country changed their rules, serving anyone regardless of race.

Math Olympics: Just like the regular Olympics, but with math instead of sports. Also, with smaller medals.

Sir Isaac Newton (1642–1727): A physicist and mathematician famous for numerous achievements, including sitting around and watching apples fall, and inventing calculus. Sophie thinks he's amazing. Julia, not so much.

reverse psychology: A method of getting people to do what you want them to by convincing them that you want the exact opposite. Very useful for extending allowances and bedtimes.

ring-tailed lemur: A primate most easily recognized by its long, black-and-white-ringed tail. Ring-tailed lemurs are native to the island of Madagascar, eat mainly plants and bugs, and occasionally get into fights, although usually with other male lemurs and not with taffy. They often sit in the sun for long periods of time, with their arms out to their sides and their bellies stretched up toward the sky, in what is known as their "sun-worshiping" position. Loud and ferocious, they make terrible pets (sorry, Lenny).

Robespierre: A surname most typically associated with Maximilien Robespierre (1758–1794), an official who ordered the execution of so many people during the French Revolution that his period of leadership is known as the Reign of Terror. Like many of his victims, he was eventually beheaded. No one knows for sure if Madame Robespierre is one of Maximilien's descendants, but chances are good that she is.

Saltwater taffy: A very sticky type of candy that needs to be pulled before it can be eaten. It is never made with either salt water or boa constrictors. See following page for a recipe.

sit-in: A nonviolent form of protest in which people sit in one place and refuse to leave until their demands are met. Very useful in changing government policy, or in ending a horrible dance recital.

topographic map: A type of map that shows how tall or short things are, from mountains to riverbeds. Not typically made out of mashed potatoes.

How to Make Madagascar Ground Boa Taffy

Saltwater taffy is almost as much fun to make as it is to eat. Since the mixture gets extremely hot, you should only try this recipe with the help of an adult.

What you'll need:

2 cups sugar
2 tablespoons cornstarch
1 cup light corn syrup
¾ cup water
2 tablespoons butter, cut into small pieces
1 teaspoon salt

1 teaspoon flavoring (such as vanilla, lemon, maple, or mint)
green food coloring
extra butter for greasing

cookie sheet with raised edges, or shallow baking dish
very large saucepan (3- to 4-quart)
wooden spoon
candy thermometer
small bowl filled with cold water
waxed paper
cooking scissors, or a butter knife, greased with butter

What to do:

1. Grease the cookie sheet or baking dish with butter and set it aside.
2. In the saucepan, mix together the sugar and cornstarch. Add the corn syrup, water, 2 tablespoons of butter, and salt.
3. Place the saucepan over medium heat, and stir constantly until the sugar dissolves and the mixture begins to boil, about 10 to 15 minutes.
4. Let the mixture continue to boil, without

stirring, and insert candy thermometer, until it reads 270°F. This will take about 15 minutes.

5. Test the mixture by spooning a small amount of it into the bowl of cold water. The mixture should solidify into thin strands that are flexible, not brittle. Remove the strands from the water. If you can form them into a ball in your hand, the mixture is not hot enough and needs to boil a while longer. If the strands bend slightly before breaking, you have reached the perfect temperature.

6. Remove the saucepan from the heat. Add the flavoring and food coloring (about 5 to 20 drops, depending on how dark you want the taffy to be), and stir gently.

7. Pour the mixture onto the cookie sheet or into the baking dish, and let it sit until it hardens slightly and is cool enough to handle, about 15 to 20 minutes.

8. Grease your hands with butter. Take about a third of the taffy mixture from the cookie sheet and pull it between your hands, stretching it out and then folding it back on itself, and stretching again. Continue to pull the taffy until it becomes lighter and has a satiny gloss, about 7 to 10 minutes. Look out for flying lemurs!

9. Roll the pulled taffy into a long, thin snake, about ½ inch in diameter, and cut it with the greased scissors or knife into 1-inch-long pieces. Repeat steps 8 and 9 until you have pulled and cut all of the taffy.

10. Let the taffy pieces sit for about 30 minutes, then wrap in small squares of waxed paper, twisting the ends.

Makes about 50 pieces

GOFISH

LISA GRAFF

What did you want to be when you grew up?
I loved math and science when I was a kid, science especially. So I always thought I'd grow up to be a doctor. That lasted until my first year of college, when I discovered I hated chemistry worse than boiled brussels sprouts. (I would later learn to adore brussels sprouts. Chemistry, however, still hasn't grown on me.)

What's your most embarrassing childhood memory?
I had many, many embarrassing moments as a kid, but this one took the cake: My middle school had a school-wide assembly at the end of each semester, during which the name of every student who had received straight As on his or her report card would be put into a hat. One name would be drawn from the hat, and that person had the honor of participating in the "money jump," which was a long, taped-together strip of dollar bills that the student had to leap across. As far

as you could jump, that's how much mone
take home. After the jump, everyone in the
count out loud as Mrs. Rouse, the lang
teacher, slapped the bills into the winner
"Twenty-six! Twenty-seven!" It was very dr
theory, it was a fantastic honor to be picked
money jump—who *wouldn't* want to earn m
good grades? But in reality, it was pretty
wracking, because most of the straight-A stu
(myself included) weren't exactly the type of kids
enjoyed showing off their long-jumping skills in fro
the entire student population.

Anyway, I'm sure you can see where this is going. A
the very end of seventh-grade (a year in which I was so
awkward that I wore stretch purple leggings almost
every day), I was called down for the money jump. And it
was even more horrible than I'd imagined it would be,
because I did not just jump badly, like I had all those
times in gym class. Oh, no. I actually *fell over*, flat on my
awkward butt. Mrs. Rouse had to help me to my feet in
front of everyone, and then she led the entire school in
loudly counting out my winnings. *"Three! Four!"* That was
it. I earned four whole dollars. I was the least- successful
money-jumper in the history of Big Bear Middle School.

What was your favorite thing about school?

I loved nearly everything about school (except for the
aforementioned money-jumping fiasco). I was one of
those rare kids who spent the whole summer looking
forward to the first day of school, anxiously picking out
an outfit and arranging my brand-new pencils *just so*
in my binder. I loved school so much, in fact, that when
I came down with strep throat the night before the first

urth grade, I was so desperate to show up to
at—even though I had spent the entire night
ng in pain—I convinced my mother to let me go,
use *I absolutely could not miss the first day of
ool*. (To this day, I'm not sure how I pulled this off—I
nk my mom must have been too tired from the night
f weeping to argue). Anyway, I got on the bus and had
an amazing first day of school . . . and went to the hospital for my tonsillectomy that very afternoon.

What was your least favorite thing about school?
The only thing I truly hated about school was P.E. I was,
and still am, a helpless athlete. Group sports were the
worst for me, because when I wasn't getting hit in the
head with a baseball (actually happened), I was busy
scoring the winning point for the wrong team in bas-
ketball (actually happened). I spent a good deal of my
growing-up years creating excuses about why I couldn't
participate in P.E.

**What were your hobbies as a kid? What are your
hobbies now?**
I loved to read as a kid, and write plays with my friends
that we'd perform for our parents. I also used to participate in my town's Old Miner's Day festivities every
summer, which celebrated the fact that Big Bear City,
the small Southern California town where I grew up,
was founded by gold miners. The most spectacular of
the Old Miner's Day events was the Miss Clementine
Pageant, in which participants would dress up in their
most authentic 1800's Old West garb. The teen girl who
was crowned Miss Clementine got to lead that year's
Old Miner's Day parade, and host several events for

local charity groups. Sadly, I never won that cov
role (although I still have my trophy for Most Authe
1990—Junior Category).

These days, I spend much less time sporting bu
tles to win trophies, and more time doing boring thin₂
like baking and bike-riding. I still love to read.

Where do you write your books?

I write my books either in my home office in my pajamas, or at a coffee shop (typically not in my pajamas).

What sparked your imagination for *Sophie Simon Solves Them All*?

I've always loved writing about characters who were a
little unusual, or who saw things from a different per-
spective than most other people. For a long time, I had
this little-girl character in my head who was insanely
smart, but who was completely incapable of communi-
cating with other children. I wrote several short exer-
cises when I was in graduate school with her as the
star, until one of my professors told me I should stop
writing about that character, "because you'll never
make a book out of it." (A lot of people told me Sophie
was too unlikeable and surly to make a good protago-
nist.) I probably should have listened to him, but luckily
for this book, I didn't!

What was your favorite book when you were a kid? Do you have a favorite book now?

I had so many favorites. My taste was all over the map.
I really loved the Old Mother West Wind books and The
Baby-Sitters Club series, as well as all the Beverly
Cleary Ramona books and everything Roald Dahl ever

t really made me fall in love with
vas *Around the World in 80 Days*,
d in the school library when I was in
made a fort in my room out of blankets,
ardboard boxes that existed for the sole
eading that book—no one was allowed
unless they were reading *Around the World*
s, and when the book was over, the fort went
he story was so spectacular to me that it de-
its own little world.

don't have a particular favorite book at the moment,
one of my favorite authors is P.G. Wodehouse. I
ver tire of reading a really funny book.

**If you could travel in time, where would you go
and what would you do?**
I'd love to go to the 1950s and visit my parents when they
were kids. They both grew up in Southern California, but
they didn't meet until high school. It would be fun to see
my grandparents as young parents, and to see how my
own parents interacted with their brothers and sisters.
(Plus, in photos, they always look stinking adorable!)

**Do you have any strange or funny habits? Did you
when you were a kid?**
I have only ever liked eating chocolate pudding with a
plastic spoon. Chocolate pudding tastes weird with a
metal spoon. I keep a stash of plastic spoons on hand
in the cutlery drawer, just in case some chocolate pudding should decide to turn up suddenly.

SQUARE FISH